MW01602773

BAKING MATTERS WORSE

RAISED AND GLAZED COZY MYSTERIES, BOOK 25

EMMA AINSLEY

SUMMER PRESCOTT BOOKS PUBLISHING

Copyright 2023 Summer Prescott Books

All Rights Reserved. No part of this publication nor any of the information herein may be quoted from, nor reproduced, in any form, including but not limited to: printing, scanning, photocopying, or any other printed, digital, or audio formats, without prior express written consent of the copyright holder.

**This book is a work of fiction. Any similarities to persons, living or dead, places of business, or situations past or present, is completely unintentional.

CHAPTER ONE

"I'm a little worried about Orson today," Maggie Sharpe whispered to her best friend and business partner, Ruby Cobb. She held a tray of plain yeast donuts ready for the glazing machine.

"What do you mean?" Ruby asked. She immediately set the large knife in her hand down and turned to her friend.

Maggie looked over her shoulder before she spoke, making sure Orson had not come back into the donut shop's kitchen. The last time she had seen him, he'd been seated at the Old Timer's table, arguing over the latest baseball statistics. Delbert was a die-hard St. Louis Cardinals fan. Normally, Orson didn't care, but today, just to be contrary, he had taken up the banner for the Kansas City Royals as if he had played for them himself.

"I saw him walking around with the coffee pot a little while ago and his step was just slower than normal," Maggie said. "His hand was shaking a little bit, too."

"Do you think he needs to go to the hospital or something?"

"No," Maggie said. "I don't think so. He just seems slower today to me."

"Do you think we're working him too hard?" Ruby asked. She folded her arms over her chest. "Maybe we should send him home for the day."

"Like we could make him go home for the day," Maggie joked. "I think we've all been a little over-worked lately, but I thought I might have him do the paperwork I was going to take care of later. That way, I can pitch in more out front while he takes it easy."

"Why don't you let me handle talking to him?" Ruby asked. "That way he thinks he is doing you a favor."

"Yeah, okay. That might make this whole thing more likely to happen," Maggie said as she nodded her head. Ruby was right. Usually, Orson couldn't be convinced to do anything unless he thought he was fulfilling his role as father figure and protector for the rest of them. It was the perfect deception.

Maggie left Ruby to her devious work and returned to the glazer to ice the rapidly cooling donuts on her tray. A few moments later, Ruby returned through the swinging door. She grinned and winked at Maggie, who was waiting close to the prep table. Orson appeared at the door not long after. His face was a little more pale than normal, but his eyes were sharp. His lips were pursed when he nodded at Maggie.

"Why don't you give those inventory sheets to me and let me go over the order for the coming week?" he muttered. "I feel like being off my feet as much as possible today, and it will give me something to do while I'm sitting there with those talkative old men."

Maggie dropped her head and sighed. "Are you sure you want to take that on?" she asked. "I mean, it would be a huge load off of my mind, but I don't want to overwhelm you."

Orson clicked his tongue at her. "You just bring those papers on out here to me as soon as you have the chance, and I will have them completed by the end of the work day. Josie is coming in at nine to take over the front anyway, so I can spend the time taking care of things."

Maggie nodded and pushed the glazed donut tray onto the cooling rack. She headed to the office and retrieved the necessary papers, a handful of pens, and a calculator. She delivered the paperwork to the table where Orson was seated. He had moved himself to the table next to the Old Timer's table and began methodically spreading the papers out in front of him.

She returned to the kitchen where Ruby was chatting with Naomi, who had taken on the running the automatic donut machines. Myra had the day off to deal with doctor's visits for her daughter, Lexi, while she battled a double ear infection and runny nose.

Maggie checked on Orson around noon when she brought out one of the boxed lunches Ruby had prepared earlier in the day. "You know, you really ought to delegate more responsibilities," Orson said to her when she set the food on the table in front of him.

"You want to handle the inventory from now on?" Maggie asked him, surprised at the idea.

Orson nodded his head. "Yes, I do, actually," he said. He sighed and gazed out the window. "I'm going to slow down eventually. Handling more paperwork helps me feel like I can still contribute even when my body tells me no."

Maggie pulled out the chair next to him and took

a seat. "You know you don't have to keep working at all," she said. She covered his hand with her own. "You can go home and rest."

"No, I can't go home and rest." Orson turned to her and looked into her eyes. "If I go home and sit down, I will never get back up."

"That's not true," Maggie said. "You live with Myra, Brooks, and Lexi. There is no way you will never get back up."

Orson cleared his throat and removed his hand from hers. "When you get a little older, my dear, you will understand that sentiment much more," he said. "Besides, there is no way I can go anywhere. You need me too much around here. You and everyone else in this donut shop, even Ruby. She's the most put together of all of you, and even she needs the old man to look out for her from time to time. So, you just figure up the new duties for me and I'll stay busy that way. Heck, if that boy of yours over in Hunter Springs needs an extra hand or two, you just let him know I can drive over that way and help."

Maggie stood up again, She leaned over and kissed Orson on the top of his snow white head. She headed back to the kitchen and began loading the dishwasher with the dirty pans from the morning's baking. "He wants to take over the paperwork entirely now," she said to Ruby as soon as she had a minute to speak to her privately.

"I've been meaning to talk to you about something," Ruby said. She gestured for Maggie to follow her into the office.

"What's going on?" Maggie asked. She felt a lump forming in her throat, hoping that the news wasn't going to be grim.

"Well, there is a baking convention coming up in the Smoky Mountains in a week," she said. "It's called the Baker's Unlimited Convention and I have our tickets already. I forgot all about them until I got an email last night wanting confirmation that we would be going."

"Just you and me?"

"For the convention, yes," Ruby said. "But thanks to a last-minute cancellation, I just found an entire log cabin in the mountains. One week's stay there will cost the same as two nights in a hotel for the two of us."

"So, what are you thinking?"

Ruby smiled. "I've added up the people who could come and sort of planned everything out, and I think there would be enough room for me, you, Myra, Naomi, and Orson, as well as Brett and Brooks if they could swing time away from their work."

Maggie walked around the desk and took a seat in the chair behind it. "Let me get this straight," she said. "You want to attend this convention for two days, bring half of our staff with us along with the two top law enforcement officers in the area, and then spend the remainder of the week in the mountains in a log cabin?"

Ruby broke into a wide grin. "I sure do," she said. "And I know for a fact that Brook's aunt has been begging to babysit, so even if those two can't come for the whole time, they can at least enjoy a little time away."

"And who is going to run our business for us while we are gone?" Maggie asked. She was almost angry with Ruby for bringing it up in the first place, mainly because she wanted to go so badly.

"I already thought of that, and I took the liberty of speaking to Bradley," Ruby said.

"Don't you think running two donut shops would be a lot for him?" She hated to think of her son suffering under the weight of running both stores, along with shuttling his small son Wyatt back and forth to daycare.

"It wouldn't be all on him. I promise," Ruby said. "He thought it was a great idea. In fact, it was his suggestion that Zeke take over the Hunter

Springs location for the week so he can run things here."

"Zeke and Bradley are going to take over the stores," Maggie thought aloud. She was starting to believe the getaway was possible.

CHAPTER TWO

One week later, Maggie pulled a rolling suitcase behind her and headed out her back door to the vehicle waiting outside. Ruby had made the decision to pay for a rideshare lift to the airport in Joplin. Together, they would fly to Tennessee and the others would meet them there the next day.

"Are you ready for the flight?" Ruby asked her. She was dressed like a tourist, from her sunglasses down to her woven oversized purse.

"I'm ready, but you look more like you're headed to the beach instead of the mountains," Maggie said.

"That's because after two days of doing nothing but talking about the latest innovations in the baking world, I intend to commune with nature."

"You live on a farm in the middle of the Ozarks,"

Maggie said. "Just how much more natural can you be?"

"I want to see bears," Ruby said. She narrowed her eyes and focused out the window past Maggie. "I want to see real Smoky Mountain black bears and I'm not leaving until I do."

"Maybe you'll see Dolly Parton," the driver said. It was the first time he had spoken since the ride began. "I hear she shows up every once in a while at her place there. Word is she comes home to the mountains sometimes just to see how things are going."

They exchanged looks and thanked the driver. They chatted about the programs involved in the convention as Maggie looked over the leaflet for the event. She was most excited about the class that offered natural and organic alternatives to some of the industries' most common flavors.

Ruby said she was excited to attend the class on creating a brand for an existing restaurant, and even suggested to Maggie that a third location might be in order. She felt a twinge of excitement at the thought but was also a little overwhelmed.

"Part of me can't believe we're actually doing this," Maggie said when they took their seats on the small plane at the airport in Joplin.

Ruby nodded. "It just happened to work out that we could go," she said. "The convention offered a discount on tickets and a few other amenities, by the way."

"So, maybe you can go see your bears at a discounted rate," Maggie said.

"Yes, because I'm using one of those discounts to rent a car at the airport when we get there, but that's not what I'm planning. I won't be seeing bears in some captive setting. I intend to drive up into those mountains and see them in person."

Their flight was uneventful. By the time they touched down in Knoxville, Maggie began to feel more relaxed. She followed Ruby through the small airport and to the car rental counter where they picked up the keys to a compact car and headed out to the parking lot. They drove an hour south to the Gatlin-burg area.

"Let's check out the cabin first, and then we can go and grab our passes at the convention center," Ruby suggested. An evening social was the only thing on the itinerary for the night, and Maggie hadn't decided if she wanted to attend or not. They had discussed attending only the sessions they were inter-ested in on the plane. Ruby told Maggie she was okay if their interests differed, too.

"I think two classes tomorrow interest me the most," Maggie declared. "Aside from that, we'll see."

Maggie felt any lingering stress melt away when Ruby turned up the winding mountain road to the cabin with the red metal roof about halfway to the top of the steep hill. Ruby slowed the car and pulled off the road onto the winding driveway. As she drove further in, the trees seemed to surround them, cutting off the rest of the world to the few acres around the cabin.

Two large decks and a patio beneath provided plenty of outdoor space. Maggie could see the deck at the back of the house, too, that housed an extra-large hot tub. She thought about the new bathing suit in her suitcase. She had purchased it for the summer but never once got the chance to use it. Maybe she would have the chance over the coming days, under the stars with Brett next to her.

"Where are our rooms?" Maggie asked the second Ruby opened the front door to the large cabin. For a minute, she thought she was seeing things. The interior of the cabin was much grander and even more gorgeous than the outside. In fact, the place could have passed for the setting of a sleek modern day western on television. A large fireplace stood in the center of the house. The chimney was made of river rock, and it extended through the main level and the second level where most of the bedrooms were.

"There is a double master bedroom," Ruby explained. "I thought it would be best for Myra and Brooks to take one and you to take another one with Brett. Will that work?"

Maggie simply smiled and nodded her head. "What about you, though?" Maggie asked. "Please don't tell me that you are going to bunk with Naomi."

"No, there are three more rooms available," Ruby said. "I'll share a bathroom with her so Orson can be comfortable on his own."

"That's pretty generous of you," Maggie said. "What do you say we retire to our rooms for a short nap? When we get up, we can decide then if we feel like going to the evening event."

"Sounds like a plan," Ruby said. She directed Maggie to the large suite on one end of the massive upstairs hallway and then headed back downstairs to one of the bedrooms on the first floor. Ruby's room opened directly to the first floor deck.

An hour later, Maggie stepped out onto the deck and surveyed the woods surrounding the cabin. She could hear the hush of the wind in the trees. Even the sounds from the highway were filtered out from the trees.

The colors in the trees had begun to change from shades of green to reds, golds, and yellows. It was early fall, and the colors would continue for weeks. Maggie was pleased when the cool breeze blew out of the woods and across her face. This was going to be a wonderful getaway.

"What are you thinking?" Ruby asked when she stepped out on the deck to join her.

"About this evening? I think we could run down there and enjoy a drink for half an hour, then head back here for a little while," she said.

Ruby placed both of her hands on the railing of the deck. She breathed in deeply and sighed. "I think that's a terrific plan," she said. "Thirty minutes of socializing and then an evening under these stars."

"This was a great idea you had," Maggie said.

"I hope so," Ruby said. "I still haven't seen a single bear yet."

"You'll see bears some time over the next few days." Maggie chuckled. "Anyway, I am going to freshen up before we go."

"Meet you in the kitchen in fifteen minutes," Ruby said.

CHAPTER THREE

Inspired by the weather, Maggie slipped boots over her favorite leggings and topped the outfit off with an oversized sweater. She pulled her hair on top of her head and added a pair of dangling earrings to complete her look.

Ruby appeared in the kitchen dressed unlike Maggie had ever seen her. Her dark green silk blouse was tucked into black cigarette pants. She looked svelte and about ten years younger than she had on the plane.

They walked down the rocky driveway to the rental car and were at the convention center in less than fifteen minutes. It was just after seven when they walked into the main lobby of the center. Maggie followed Ruby to the registration table where the hostess found their names and offered them each a name tag. Inside the hall, the vast space was open aside from a half-dozen drink and appetizer stations set up for attendees to mill about. Maggie accepted two champagne flutes from a passing waiter. She handed one of the glasses to Ruby and sipped her own. It was the only drink she intended to have.

They walked around the room, nodding politely to several people as they passed. A tall blond man approached them and smiled. "And where are the two of you from?" he asked. His words were clipped and precise. Maggie wondered where his accent was from.

"We own a chain of donut shops in the Ozarks," Ruby said.

"Oh, yes," the blond man smiled. Stanley Riles was the name on his shiny blue blazer. "I am quite familiar with the area. One of my first jobs was in Branson."

"One of your first jobs? What do you do now?" Maggie asked.

Stanley smiled. He opened one side of his jacket and pulled a pamphlet out from the inside pocket.

"I'm a business consultant," he said with a wide grin. "I have a knack of transforming businesses into brands."

"Brands?" Ruby asked. "Are you the presenter for the 'Business Brands' class tomorrow morning?"

Stanley's grin widened even more. "I am indeed," he said. "I take it the two of you signed up for it?"

Ruby nodded her head. "I've read your blog for years and I look forward to your presentation."

"And I look forward to seeing your face when I present," Stanley said. He picked up Ruby's hand and kissed it. Maggie bit the inside of her lip. The move was something she had seen in the movies a dozen times but seeing it in person made it seem silly and staged.

"That was interesting," Maggie said when Stanley was out of earshot.

"It was something," Ruby said. "Even so, I think the class will be good. This guy is paid a whole lot of money to transform struggling businesses. And he is very good at it."

"But he's going to give away his secrets in a convention workshop?" Maggie asked.

Ruby shook her head. "He's going to give his general guidelines, but he works his magic one on one," she said. "Are you going to attend class with me?"

"I thought about it," Maggie said. "I want to make it to the 'Baking Naturally' class, too. I'd like to learn more about the movement to replace ingredients with more natural, healthier alternatives."

"I'm interested in that class as well," Ruby said. She watched Stanley from the other side of the room. He was surrounded by a trio of women, all well within their late sixties, while a dark-haired, slim younger woman moved around him. "I wonder if that's his wife or something."

Maggie watched as well. "I was thinking she was his assistant or secretary," she said. She followed Ruby to one of the hors d'oeuvres stations. She picked up a smoked salmon canape and nibbled on it. It might have been the champagne, but she giggled a little when she thought it was weird that a baking convention was not featuring baked goods.

They walked around the hall for a little while. Maggie walked away from Ruby for a few moments. She exchanged pleasantries with a few more people, including Penelope, the owner of a donut shop from the St. Louis area. She was excited to spend a little more time with the woman. There was a lot she thought she could learn from someone with a thriving business in such a large area.

"Are you ready to go?" Ruby asked her a bit later. "I think our thirty minutes are up and I am not feeling the need to visit the rest of these stations."

"I'm ready to go," Maggie said. They set their champagne flutes down and headed for the door.

"Did you meet anyone interesting tonight, aside from Stanley?" Ruby asked her.

"I met a woman named Penelope from St. Louis with a donut shop of her own," Maggie said. "She's going to be in the 'Baking Naturally' class tomorrow, too."

"Nice," Ruby said. "I met three more people interested in Stanley's class. I think one of them owns a bakery close by around here somewhere."

"And they were all interested in Stanley's branding class?" Maggie asked.

"Very interested in it," Ruby said. "I'm a little overwhelmed by his popularity, to be honest with you." She pulled the car out of the parking lot and headed back toward the mountains.

"I thought you followed this guy online," Maggie asked.

"I do, but these people are almost like groupies," Ruby said with a chuckle. "They buy his books and follow his YouTube channel."

"He wrote a book?"

Ruby nodded her head and laughed as she drove. "A book? This guy has seven books in print," she said.

"All about branding baking businesses?" Maggie asked in disbelief.

"Exactly," Ruby said. "I still want to attend his class, but let's find our seats in the back."

"Agreed," Maggie said. She closed the car door behind her and headed for the front door of the cabin right behind Ruby. Once they were inside, both women went straight for their bedrooms to change into more comfortable clothes.

"I think I'd like to enjoy a glass of red wine on the deck before going to bed," Maggie announced when she joined Ruby in the spacious kitchen.

"I plan to do the same, except white wine is my choice for the night," Ruby said. She poured herself a glass and set the red wine bottle on the counter for Maggie.

With their glasses in hand, they headed out to the deck overlooking the woods. The sun had set but the moonlight illuminated the trees and the yard around the cabin.

"Did you see that?" Maggie asked when her glass was half empty. She pointed to the backyard where a dozen white Adirondack chairs were set in a circle around a large, iron fire pit.

"I did," Ruby said. "It sort of reminds me of home."

Maggie headed for bed an hour later. She felt the magic of the mountains lull her into a restful sleep. She woke early the following morning and took an unrushed shower, dressed for the day, and headed downstairs to the smell of coffee. Ruby was already awake and had a small pan on the stove when Maggie joined her.

"I thought we might enjoy a quick omelet before we head over to the convention center," she said.

"Sounds about perfect," Maggie said with a smile. She accepted the mug of coffee Ruby handed over to her and took a seat at the counter bar.

They ate breakfast and headed for the convention center next. Maggie was excited when she saw the crowd of people gathered in the convention hall. Just as the night before, they checked in with a hostess near the front and placed new nametags on their shirts. This time, there was a booklet with class descriptions and biographies of each of the presenters with the name tag.

Maggie flipped through the book. She leaned over to Ruby. "I didn't realize that this convention lasts another three days," she said.

Ruby nodded as she walked. "The classes repeat after two days," she said. "When I registered with them they said the demand was so high the presenters agreed to offer their classes twice. I signed us up early so we could enjoy the rest of the week."

"And that was the best plan ever," Maggie said. As much as she looked forward to the classes she was about to take, she could not wait to see Brett arrive at the log cabin.

"Looks like your natural baking class is first," Ruby said.

"I don't mind sitting toward the front of this class," Maggie said when they entered the large conference room. A kitchen area had been set up across the front of the room. Portable glass display cases held cupcakes and pastries and donuts of all kinds. The presenter was already up front shuffling around her notes and checking on several things in the model kitchen.

If she hadn't been there, Maggie would have gone to the front just to make sure the items in the display cases were real. From her vantage point, everything looked like a prop for a gourmet baking show. She was shocked at the vibrant colors in the displays.

From the description, everything prepared in the class would be free of additives and preservatives. In fact, everything there was supposed to be made only from natural ingredients. Ruby chose the end of the fourth row and took a seat. Maggie flipped through her booklet and waited for the class to begin.

The presenter stepped to the middle of the front and adjusted her microphone headset before she began her introduction. Maggie was instantly captivated by the woman's description of the baking world made healthier. She had to check the booklet again for the woman's name. "Cora Kennedy," she whispered.

"What did you say?" Ruby leaned over and asked her quietly.

"I was just reading the name of the presenter," Maggie said. "I completely forgot to look."

"You should get one of her cookbooks," Ruby suggested. "I think I own two myself."

"Is this legit, then?" Maggie asked. "Her whole approach?"

Ruby nodded. "It is, but there's a catch," she said.

"Is this a waste of time? Be honest."

"Not at all," Ruby said. "For us, this makes a lot of sense."

Half an hour later, Maggie understood Ruby's words. There was no secret to baking with natural ingredients, and Ruby was right that the concept Cora suggested was right up their alley. The secret was to prepare with the most natural ingredients possible, and then to serve the baked goods as soon as possible.

Under her plan, there would be no day-old cakes or cupcakes or donuts. Everything would be wasted at the end of the day.

Maggie felt a little disappointed that the purported method was that simple, but she was enthralled by some of the donut varieties the class offered. She raised her hand immediately when the presenter asked for volunteers to try one of the three donut varieties she had in the display cases in the front.

Maggie was given a sample of a sweet corn and blueberry donut, which she promptly shared with Ruby.

"What do you think?" Cora asked her after the first bite.

"I think I'm shocked these flavors could come together like this," Maggie said.

Cora turned her attention to the rest of the group. "The lady is right," she said. "No one would expect a corn donut to find its way into the display cases at a donut shop. But here we have a corn custard with a blueberry glaze inside a lemon and corn shortbread."

"That's incredible," Maggie said.

Cora smiled and turned her attention to the second variety, a chile and chocolate donut. The third was a southeast Asian coffee-flavored donut. At the end of the class, several of Cora's assistants passed around boxes with each of the other baked goods she had featured. Maggie walked to the next class poking around in the box for a taste of the coffee donut. She decided she would leave it to Ruby to sample the hot pepper donut.

They walked through the convention center to another large space in the back. This time, the conference room was arranged like a theater, with rows of chairs in a semicircle pattern and large, drop-down screens overhead. Maggie followed Ruby to a middle row where they chose their seats at the end.

"I'm not too interested in watching all of this from a screen," Ruby said when she sat down.

"Yeah, but if these groupies get a little rowdy, I would like the option to leave," Maggie teased. Ruby rolled her eyes and opened the booklet once more. Maggie scanned her own booklet for a few more details about the class, and the instructor.

From his bio, Maggie was shocked that Stanley Riles would have a core group of fans loyal enough to be his groupies. He was charming to be sure, but his looks weren't so remarkable that she could see the draw. He was a former high school history teacher who wrote a book about productivity, took on a few consultation jobs, and became an overnight sensation.

He still looked the part of a teacher. He was tall

and lanky with thinning blond hair and pale skin. But his eyes seemed to sparkle when he spoke with anyone. Maggie noted he was especially effervescent around women. Something about him reminded her of a leading man in an old movie. It was all a bit too cliché for her liking.

She leaned over in her chair to speak with Ruby but stopped when the lights went down. Colorful beams of light began to dance around the front of the conference room. Music boomed over the speakers and a misting machine spewed fog straight up the center of the front.

"Here he is! Stan "The Man" Riles to teach you how to become the star of your own business," a recorded emcee voice said.

Maggie and Ruby exchanged looks. Stanley walked out from the fog with his hands waving high over his head. Maggie was reminded of a star quarterback emerging from the locker room during a televised football game.

Ruby leaned over to her when the hyping act continued for another full minute. "I think I made a big mistake," she said.

"Do you want to leave?" Maggie asked. She was more than happy to vacate her seat at that moment.

"Yeah," Ruby said with a sigh. "I wanted to listen

to what he had to say in person, but if this is a preview, I think I'll skip it. I don't think this is the sort of branding I need to hear more about." Ruby stood up and turned quickly to head toward the back of the conference room. Maggie followed right behind her.

Ruby hit one of the doors in the back with two hands. She pushed the door open with a flourish and waited for Maggie on the other side. Right away the dark haired younger woman from the night before stepped in front of the two of them.

"Where do you think you're going?" she asked. Both hands went to her thin hips.

"We're not staying for the presentation," Ruby said matter of factly.

"You aren't supposed to be able to leave," the woman said. Her pale skin colored slightly when she spoke. She was clearly unsettled by their presence. Her voice had an odd, almost robotic cadence. "Those doors are supposed to be locked once the presentation begins."

"Well, they weren't locked," Maggie said from behind Ruby. "Now, if you will excuse us, we have to go."

"You cannot go," the woman argued. She didn't even attempt to move out of their way.

Maggie searched for a name tag on the woman's clothing but found nothing. "We are leaving, and you need to move out of our way." She stepped closer to Ruby who appeared speechless.

"No, no," the woman repeated herself. "You have to turn right around and go back in there."

"What is your name?" Ruby spoke to the woman at last.

"My name? I'm Rebecca Concord, and I need you to turn around and go back in there!" Her voice rose a little to a whine.

"We are not interested, thank you, Rebecca," Maggie said. She grabbed Ruby's hand, pulling her around the woman. Her shoulder connected with her as she walked by.

Rebecca continued to argue as they made their way down the hall and headed to the main part of the convention center.

"Let's just keep walking until we get out of here," Ruby said when they entered the main hall. "I don't fancy answering any questions about why we want to go."

"I'm with you," Maggie said. She released Ruby's hand as they walked swiftly across the large space.

Aside from the hostess seated in front of the table

near the entrance they encountered no one as they left.

"That was strange," Ruby said when they reached the rental car at last. "I mean, you and I have had our fair share of strange experiences, but that one really stands out to me."

"Me, too," Maggie said. "I don't know if the fog machine or the odd behavior of the woman outside was more cringeworthy, but I am glad we didn't stay for the rest of that."

Ruby nodded as she backed the car out of the parking spot. "At least we got something out of the baking presentation," she said. "Right now, I say let's check in with everyone else and see how soon they'll be here."

"And we can grab lunch on the way back to the cabin and eat outside," Maggie added.

CHAPTER FOUR

"We're on our way now," Brett told her when she called him as soon as they arrived back at the cabin. He was alone in his own vehicle, following behind Brooks and Myra in their large SUV. Naomi and Orson rode along with Brooks.

"How do you like the truck so far?" Maggie asked. After driving only his 1980s muscle car for years, Brett broke down a month before and purchased a Dodge pickup truck. The trip to the Smoky Mountains was his first long drive in it.

"It's actually really nice," Brett said. Maggie could hear the smile in his voice. "I think you're going to enjoy the trip back."

"I hope so," she said. He ended the phone call with the promise to see her in a few hours. Maggie set her phone on the nightstand next to her bed and threw a sweater over her tank top and yoga pants before heading out of her room.

Ruby was in the kitchen pouring coffee into a large cup when Maggie found her. "Did you hear from Brett?" she asked.

"Yeah, he said they'll be here in a few hours," Maggie said. "Brooks is driving everyone else out."

Ruby nodded her head. "I wondered if Brett would wind up with Orson."

Maggie shook her head. "Orson called the new truck a cursed vehicle in need of a step ladder," she smiled. "But he's going to have to deal with it on the ride home."

"Sounds about right coming from Orson." Ruby laughed and set the spoon she had stirred her coffee with down in the sink. "What are you going to do the rest of the morning?"

"Well," Maggie said. "I think I might hang out on the deck with a cup of tea for a while."

"I think that's an excellent idea," Ruby said. They headed for the deck together and each took a seat. They chatted for just a few moments when Ruby sat up quickly. "I think I hear my phone ringing." She set her coffee down and rushed back inside the kitchen.

Maggie rested her head on the back of the chair

and propped her feet on the ottoman. She inhaled the woodsy aroma from the trees around her. Somewhere close by a pair of squirrels chased each other around in the treetops.

She jumped up quickly when Ruby raced back outside holding her phone in her hand.

"What's going on?" Maggie asked her. Ruby's face was drained and pale.

"I just got a phone call from the registrar at the convention center," she said. "They were calling to let me know that the convention has been canceled."

"Canceled?" Maggie asked. "Why did they cancel it? We were just there."

Ruby frowned "Because there was a death."

"What are you talking about?" Maggie asked. "Who died?"

Ruby sat down hard on her chair. "I can't believe I'm going to say this, but Stanley Riles was found dead after his last class."

"Are you talking about the last class we just were at? That class? He died after that class?"

Ruby nodded her head slowly. "Apparently he keeled over right after the end of the class."

"I wonder if he had a heart attack or something?" Maggie said. She was seated upright and felt her heart racing.

"The registrar seems to think it was a bit more sinister than that," Ruby said. "He said the convention presenters immediately suspended their contract and began packing everything up. He thought that was quite suspicious until the local news began calling for a statement about Stanley's murder."

"The registrar heard about the murder from the local news?" Maggie asked.

"He knew about the death but not that it was a murder until the reporter said something to him about it," Ruby said. "The presenters are separate from the convention centers, of course. Anyway, he was pretty ruffled about it."

"Seems like you are, too," she said. "Are you okay?"

Ruby shook her head. "I am, I suppose," she said. "I just can't believe the same guy we walked out on died right after we were there."

"Me either," Maggie said.

"He had such a big personality. I can't believe someone would want to kill him. He might have been cheesy and weird, but he was not exactly the type to incur anger or rivalry."

"Yeah," Maggie agreed. "Who knocks off a branding personality?"

"Right. I can't imagine Stanley Riles would

inspire enough wrath to cause anyone to want to hurt him," Ruby said.

Maggie stood up and stretched her arms over her head. "So much for a relaxing getaway," she said.

"What do you mean by that?" Ruby asked. "We were done with the convention anyway. It's not really our problem."

"Maybe so." Maggie pointed toward the driveway. "But it looks like the county sheriff just showed up to make it our problem."

CHAPTER FIVE

Maggie sat back down as two uniformed officers approached the deck. She sat still and waited for them to come up the steps and say their piece.

"Why did you sit back down as soon as you saw us coming?" the first deputy asked the minute he stepped up on the deck. Maggie was a little taken back that he spoke before introducing himself.

"I sat down because my significant other is a county sheriff back home in Missouri, and if he was approaching two strangers, I think it would be safer for everyone if they just sat down and let him approach," she said.

"That's a little weird, don't you think?" the first deputy asked his partner.

"No, man." He shook his head. "I wish more

people felt that way. By the way, I'm Deputy Gilley and he's Deputy Faust."

"What can we do for you?" Ruby asked.

"First, what are your names?" Deputy Faust asked. The question was less of a demand at least.

"My name is Maggie Sharpe, and I'm a business owner from Dogwood Mountain, Missouri."

"And I am her business partner and friend, Ruby Cobb, from the same town."

"Why are you two here?" Deputy Faust asked.

Deputy Gilley rolled his eyes. He was the younger of the two by far and seemed to be less inspired by his own greatness. "They're in a rental cabin in the Smokies," he said. "I don't think they're here to study the cosmos."

"You were a part of the Baker's Unlimited Convention, right?" Deputy Faust asked, eyeing his partner.

Maggie nodded. "Our business is a small chain of donut shops, and we thought attending the convention would be nice," she said.

"We left at the beginning of the Stanley Riles class this morning," Ruby blurted out.

"Okay." Deputy Gilley held up his hand to stop Faust from speaking. "Why did you leave at the beginning?"

"Because it was more like a concert than a symposium on business branding," she said. "I don't want to speak for Maggie, but the truth is, I wasn't interested in that sort of a class. It was all personality and I decided to get up and leave. It wasn't what I signed up for."

"And what about you?" Deputy Faust asked Maggie.

"The business branding class wasn't my first choice anyway," she said. "I was just there because Ruby had gone to my natural baking class right before then."

"Did anything happen while you were there?" Deputy Gilley asked, seemingly more concerned than before.

Maggie nodded her head. She glanced over at Ruby before she spoke. "When we left the room, there was a younger woman standing right outside the doors," she said. "Her name was Rebecca. Rebecca Concord, if I remember right. She tried to block us from leaving."

"What do you mean by that exactly?" Deputy Gilley pressed.

"I mean, she literally stood in front of us and tried to make us go back inside," Maggie explained.

"She was pretty insistent that no one could just

walk away and leave one of Stanley's classes," Ruby said.

"Were you on a first name basis with Mr. Riles?" Deputy Faust asked.

Ruby shook her head. "Not at all, although he did kiss my hand at the social event last night," she said. "But those were her words, the younger woman's. She said we couldn't leave one of Stanley's classes."

"Why did he kiss your hand?" Deputy Gilley asked.

Ruby shook her head. "He was just making the rounds at the social event before the convention," she replied. "Trust me. I wasn't the only person he flirted with."

"Do you consider that to be flirting?" Deputy Faust asked her. He propped his leg up on the deck railing and rested his elbow on his knee.

"In this case, I do," Ruby said. "It was all in his face and his mannerisms. What do you think, Maggie?"

Maggie nodded her head. "Flirting. Definitely."

"And after you left the class, where did you go?"

"Here," Maggie and Ruby said at the same time.

"You didn't go anywhere or grab some lunch?" Deputy Faust asked.

Ruby shook her head. "No, I made us lunch when we came back," she said.

"How long are the two of you in town?" Deputy Faust asked next.

"Till next week," Maggie said. "We have more friends coming this evening."

"And who are those people?"

"Do we need to know that?" Deputy Gilley asked.

"Yes, we need to know."

"Okay, well, three of them are our employees from our main donut shop location," Maggie said. "The other two are in law enforcement, and before you ask, I don't think you'll have any problems with them." Her face was hardened with frustration.

"Noted," Deputy Faust said. He hooked his thumbs inside his tactical vest.

"Thanks for the information, ladies," Deputy Gilley said, shaking his head as he followed his partner back to their vehicle.

CHAPTER SIX

Maggie watched while the deputies pulled out of the driveway and headed down the road. She sat back in her chair and stared at the side of the cabin. "I wonder if this is a true log cabin," she said.

"That's what you're wondering right now, after all of that?" Ruby chuckled.

"No, I mean it," Maggie said. She stood up and walked to the side of the cabin. She ran her hand along the siding. "I think it is a genuine log cabin."

"I agree," Ruby said from her seat. "That's not just siding."

Maggie dropped her hands to her sides and sighed. "I just wanted this to be a good vacation, you know?"

"I know, and I think it will be, especially once

everyone else gets here," Ruby said. "In the meantime, how about we have a little experiment?"

"An experiment?" Maggie asked. "For science or something?"

Ruby shook her head. "No, no. I'm talking about making those sweet corn and blueberry donuts while we're here." She stood up and walked slowly toward the kitchen door. "I just placed a grocery delivery order. It should be here in thirty minutes."

"You did?" Maggie asked in disbelief.

"I did." Ruby smiled. "I just thought that after the convention turned out to be such a bust, we should at least make some use of our time while we're here. We can relax for sure, but it might be fun to experiment with a new donut flavor and spring it on everyone when they get here."

Maggie nodded her head. "I agree that it would be fun, but you're not the least bit curious about Stanley's death? You don't want to look into things, even a little bit?"

"Not if you paid me," Ruby said and laughed. "Now, help me figure out what this kitchen has in it and whether or not we can pull this new donut off."

Maggie followed Ruby into the large kitchen. They opened cabinets high and low and began pulling out dishes and small appliances. Maggie found an electric skillet and a hand mixer. She pulled out a double boiler and a large whisk.

Half an hour later, Maggie stood at the large stove top. She stirred heavy cream and sweet corn kernels and then added egg yolks and additional whole eggs with sugar. After the custard was mixed together, she cooled it slightly and began her blueberry glaze on another burner. After the custard cooled, she whirred it in the blender Ruby found and handed the mixture over to Ruby who had whipped up corn shortbread for the donuts.

A couple hours after that, Maggie picked the newly made donut up and savored the interesting flavors while she watched a pair of birds dancing in the trees overhead.

"Well? What's the verdict?" Ruby asked her.

"Definitely a new menu item," Maggie nodded her head and spoke around a mouthful of donut.

"But I think this might be a little too complicated as a permanent addition to the menu,' Ruby said.

Maggie nodded her head enthusiastically. "These are very labor intensive."

Ruby settled back and enjoyed her own donut. From her seat across the deck, Maggie could see that there was something more on her mind. "You seem so lost in thought," she said after a few minutes.

"I'm thinking about the idea of taking the donut shop in new and different directions," Ruby said. "Which was why I was excited for Stanley's class in the beginning."

"I knew you were thinking about him!" Maggie said.

"Fair." Ruby nodded. "But I wasn't thinking about how to solve his case like you probably were."

Maggie grinned. "I want to hear your thoughts about the donut shop."

Ruby stood up and moved to the deck railing. She gazed over at Maggie and smiled. "I want to take the food truck out a little more often," she said.

"I like that idea," Maggie said.

"We have all of these specialty donuts we come up with and they are always a huge menu hit but adding them long term is never sustainable because of the time it takes away from the normal menu items," Ruby began.

"Exactly," Maggie agreed.

"We know these special varieties are good sellers, so, why don't we set the food truck up to offer them? We can have one day per week, probably on the weekend, where we have a selection of them available at the food truck."

"I love it." Maggie clasped her hands together in

front of her. "We can draw more people in on the weekends when we are traditionally a little slower, too." She never could figure out why a donut shop was slower on the weekends, but for them, it was true.

"I think we ought to hire someone else and put Naomi in charge a little more often, so we don't burn out," Ruby suggested. "Myra is around but not as often as she'd expected to be after having Lexi. I think it would be good to spread out everyone's time a little more, too."

Once again, Maggie found herself quickly nodding her head. "I really think that's a good idea."

"I am glad you think so, because the other part I think we ought to look into doing is expanding the use of the food truck," Ruby continued. "I think we ought to advertise the truck to businesses for different events, all across the state."

Maggie listened carefully. Her mind began to play through the scenarios. "Instead of the festivals and fairs we already go to?"

"No, in addition to it," she said. "What are we really talking about? Maybe, a half dozen events per year? I think we ought to keep that up, but also take this very specialized menu and offer the donut truck at smaller venues, like corporate events, weddings, maybe even baby showers or school events."

Maggie thought about Ruby's words for a good long time before she spoke. "Instead of opening a new location, you want to take the food truck out more often? I think that means we're going to need to put someone in charge of it, full time."

"You and I are both on the same page with that," Ruby said. "I was really thinking about Myra for that role. She could use the flexibility."

"We probably ought to talk to her about it while she's here," Maggie suggested. "Naomi, too."

"I think now is a great time. If they're even half as excited as I am about this then we're in good shape."

CHAPTER SEVEN

"It's so good to see you," Brett said when he bounded out of the pickup truck a few hours later. He picked Maggie up around her waist and swung her a half-turn before he set her back on the ground and gave her a long kiss.

"You sound like you haven't seen a woman in a year, Sheriff," Orson grumbled. He walked around staring into the sky overhead. "I don't see any mountains."

"That's because it's dark, Orson," Ruby said flatly. "You guys arrived after sunset when it's a little hard to see the mountains all around us."

"I'm quite aware what time it is, young lady," Orson said. "And it's time for you to show me to my room. I'm very tired, you know."

Ruby walked down the deck steps to the ground below. She took Orson by the hand and helped him up the steps. He muttered under his breath as they went.

Maggie shook her head and laughed. "How was the ride here with Orson in the back seat, Brooks?" she asked.

Brooks held his wife's hand and gazed up at the cabin. "Who told you he sat in the back seat? Because that man sat in the front seat the entire journey here."

"And he made sure you knew how to drive correctly," Myra said. "He also made sure that we knew not only the right streets to turn onto, but which ones were wrong and why."

"The entire trip?" Maggie asked.

"From the second we left the house," Brooks said with a plastic smile.

"But we love him," Myra said, wearing the same smile.

"We all love him," Brett said. "But I have to admit that I'm happy I was alone."

"It is so nice and cool out here," Naomi said, changing the subject. She walked close to the edge of the light from the front porch and gazed upward. "I think Orson is crazy. I can see the trees and mountains!"

They spent a few minutes chatting, and then

Maggie followed the rest of them back inside the cabin so she could show each one to their room.

"Anyone up for a late night fire?" Ruby asked after she returned from getting Orson settled into his room. "We have some experimental donuts to share and a nifty looking circle of chairs."

"If I don't need a gun and I don't need a badge, a dunk in a cold river sounds good," Brett said.

"Amen to that, but I would have to add a sippy cup and a car seat." Brooks laughed. He led his wife to the circle of wooden chairs and sat in the first one he reached. Ruby stepped between two chairs and made fast work of lighting the fire.

"Does it ever occur to anyone else that Ruby is always the one who gets the fires going?" Brett asked. "I suppose that means if we ever wind up with an unexplained arson in the county, we'll know where to start looking."

"This guy does not get served here," Ruby shouted. "No beer or donuts."

"That's not fair." Brett folded his arms and put on a show of pouting.

"That's okay, man," Brooks said. "I got you!" He picked up a beer from the small cooler and tossed it at him. Brett caught the bottle in mid-air.

"Come to the Smokies, find out who your friends

are," Brett said. Without a word of warning, Ruby walked by, grabbed the beer out of his hand, and shook it up to the point bubbles bounced around inside.

"Enjoy that beer," Ruby said with a smile and walked to the other side of the circle to take her seat.

Brooks, Naomi, and Myra burst out laughing. Defeated, Brett set the beer down on the armrest where it would stay until the bubbles died down. Maggie poured herself a glass of wine from the bottle she had placed in the cooler along with the beer.

"How was the convention?" Naomi asked when she took her own seat. She held out her empty wine glass while Maggie poured for her.

"That is not the right question to ask," Ruby said.

"That's a strange answer," Myra said. "Did something happen?"

Ruby and Maggie exchanged glances. "You might say that," Maggie said. "For starters, the one class Ruby wanted to attend turned out to be more like a multi-level marketing conference."

"Complete with a fog machine and laser lights," Ruby added with a groan.

"That's terrible," Myra said. "But if these donuts came from the conference, I would call it successful."

"The donuts came from the one good class we

attended," Maggie said. "But laser lights aren't the worst part."

"Now you have me intrigued," Brett said. "What happened?"

"The man who made the presentation with all of the bells and whistles? Yeah, he keeled over dead during the class," Ruby said. "And they canceled tomorrow."

"While you were there?" Brooks asked.

"Fortunately, we had just left," Maggie said.

"But trying to leave was a whole other story," Ruby said.

"You better just start spilling that tea," Naomi said. "And don't stop until we know what you know."

"I will, but I am going to need more wine first," Maggie said. She topped off her glass and settled back in her chair. "There was a woman, this younger girl who seemed to hang on the victim's every word when we were at the social event last night. We found out her name is Rebecca Concord. Anyway, when we got up to leave the class, she tried to physically block us from leaving."

"Yeah, almost like she couldn't conceive of the idea of us not wanting to stay and watch his presentation," Ruby added.

"Was she serious?" Brooks asked.

"Serious enough that she physically stood in front of us and basically ordered us to go back inside," Ruby said.

Brett narrowed his eyes. "I'm sorry that happened, guys. I know you were excited about that class."

Maggie looked from Ruby to Brett. She wondered when they might have discussed Ruby's thoughts about the convention. The time period from first hearing about the convention and the idea to travel together to the Smoky Mountains had been quite short.

"I was looking forward to the class but turns out it was nothing like I thought it was going to be," Ruby said.

"Seriously? Laser lights and a fog machine," Brooks asked. "That sounds hilarious."

"A single fog machine? Oh, no. I would say there had to be at least three or four," Maggie said.

They sat together under the moonlight, listening to the wind in the trees. Somewhere in the darkness Maggie heard the call of an elk up the mountain and wondered what else she would hear if she remained out there all night.

The best part was the circle of people gathered around the fire, especially the man to her right. She gazed at Brett who was engaged in a rigorous retelling of a work mishap, starring Brooks and a runaway poodle. Maggie spread her fingers between his and held tightly.

An hour later, the fire had about died out. Myra yawned and Naomi stood up. "As much as I appreciate the fire out here, I want to head for bed," she said.

"I'm right there with you," Myra said.

The rest of them stood up as Ruby and Brett put out the fire the rest of the way. "What are we doing in the morning?" Brooks asked as they headed for the log cabin. "I'm sorry your convention is canceled but I'm glad we'll have more time with you two."

"Pancakes," Ruby said. "I vote we get up early and head into town for a real Smoky Mountain breakfast."

CHAPTER EIGHT

"Why can't we make pancakes here?" Orson muttered. He stood in the kitchen between Brooks and Brett early the following morning.

"Maybe some of us don't want to cook while we're here," Maggie said.

"You cooked yesterday," Orson reminded her. "You made those donuts for everybody."

"We did, but that was a work-related experiment," Ruby countered. "Listen, Orson. If you don't want to go with us, please just relax and enjoy yourself while we're gone."

"No, I don't really want to be alone," Orson admitted at last. "I just don't see the need to be up this early in the morning. You all don't want to cook while you're here, so why are you in such a hurry to get up for the day?"

"You obviously forgot how early these ladies get out of bed to open the donut shop every day," Brett said on his way out of the kitchen.

"Yeah, seven is like sleeping until ten for the rest of us," Ruby agreed.

Maggie followed Brett to his new pickup truck and climbed in the passenger side. Naomi joined them and everyone else piled in with Myra and Brooks. The drive to the pancake house was about fifteen minutes. Maggie took in the sights on the way to town.

"I'm surprised Ruby didn't want to drive," Brett said.

"I'm not," Maggie said, still staring out the window. "She's looking for bears."

"Bears?" Naomi's voice rose. "I'm so glad I'm not riding with them."

"Yeah, bears." Maggie laughed.

Brett was silent for a moment. "You're serious," he said. "She's looking for bears?"

Maggie turned to him this time. "I'm completely serious," she said. "She said seeing a bear was the one thing she had to do while we were all here."

"Okay. Bears," Brett said. He lowered his head

and gazed upward. "I'm not here to see the bears. That's what I'm here to see." Maggie followed his gaze up the mountain. High above them she could see the long tendrils of mist rising toward the sky.

"Yeah, me too," Naomi said.

"Absolutely, for me too. I'm not looking for bears one bit," Maggie agreed.

The parking lot of the restaurant was packed with cars and trucks. Maggie felt a twinge of excitement when she opened the truck door. It was not a common occurrence for her to have the chance to go out to eat with Brett and her friends, let alone for breakfast. The tantalizing aromas of coffee, bacon, and maple syrup filled the air. Maggie looked up at the mountains looming overhead when they walked into the crowded restaurant.

After a brief delay, they were escorted to a large, round booth near tall windows on the far side of the pancake house. Maggie was glad she had the chance to gaze out at the mountains from inside the restaurant as she ate.

"It smells like a donut shop in here," Orson muttered when they squeezed into the booth.

"Aside from the bacon, I would have to agree," Brooks said.

"Well, we take that as a compliment," the perky

waitress waiting for their drink orders replied. She scurried off to the kitchen to retrieve their coffee and orange juice orders. Orson scowled after her.

"You have to love these southerners and their little accents," he said.

Myra, Brooks, and Naomi burst into laughter. Maggie bit her lip to keep from joining in.

"What?" Orson asked. He stared at them. "What did I say that was so funny? You've never been to Tennessee before?"

"Orson," Myra said at last. She reached across the table and placed her hand on his. "We're from the Ozarks. Do you think they sound all that much different from where we're from?"

"It's true," Brooks said. "About once a week, I have someone making comments about how the accents down there drive them insane. And then they ask me why I don't have the same accent."

"Same thing happens to Bradley," Brett added.

"It does?" Maggie asked. She was surprised that he knew something about her son she didn't know first. "When did you talk to Bradley about that?"

Brett shrugged. "What do you think I do when I'm in Hunter Springs?" he asked with a chuckle. "I stop in there all the time for coffee."

"Brett Mission, I am shocked," Ruby said in mock horror. "You have been cheating on us!"

Maggie ignored the chuckles from the rest of the table. "What did Bradley say about his accent?" she asked

"Oh, just that people like to point out that he really doesn't have one, and that usually prompts a discussion about his years in the Navy and how he lost any accent he might have had during that time," Brett said.

The waitress returned with a large, round tray filled with coffee cups and two large decanters, as well as glasses of juice for each of them.

"Do I have an accent?" Maggie asked quietly.

"Only a little," the waitress replied with a wink. She pulled a small notebook out from her apron pocket and began to ask each of their orders.

"I didn't think I had much of an accent," Maggie mumbled after the waitress left once more. She picked up her spoon and stirred a small amount of sugar into her coffee cup.

"You are really bothered by the notion that you have an accent, aren't you?" Naomi asked.

"No, it doesn't bother me," Maggie said. "It just surprised me, that's all. I thought I sounded like everyone else."

"Like who? Because where we're from, most people sound a little like the folks here," Ruby said.

"You know, like the people on the news," Maggie said. "That sort of everywhere accent."

"I did notice quite a few people at the convention had odd accents," Ruby said. "Including Stanley. I just couldn't place where he was from."

Maggie nodded her head, grateful to focus on someone else's accent for a change. "Yeah, I picked up on that, too," she said. "It sounded part Bostonian or something else on the east coast."

"And part German or something else," Ruby added. "I don't know where the guy was from."

"I still don't get why you two left that convention," Orson muttered. "Isn't that the whole reason we came out here in the first place?"

"No, man." Brooks smiled. He waved his hand in a small circle in front of him. "This is the whole reason we came out here."

"But seriously," Ruby said. "We left the convention because the class we attended with Stanley Riles looked nothing like we expected."

"You said something about fog machines and laser lights," Naomi said.

Maggie nodded. "And we weren't kidding," she

said. "We walked in there, took our seats, and suddenly it felt like we were at the circus."

"Or some Las Vegas magic show," Ruby said. "This guy was already kind of a weirdo the first night we met him at the social hour for the convention."

"Yeah, he acted more like a cheesy Vegas magician than a professional business consultant ready to tell you all about how to brand your business," Maggie added.

"Maybe that was part of his presentation," Brett said.

"What do you mean?" Maggie turned slightly toward him.

"I mean, maybe that whole cheesy act was part of his presentation in the first place, making the point that you have to develop a personality in order to stand out in the business world," he said.

"If that was the case, there was a little something lost in translation," Ruby said with a laugh. "I've read his blog for two years and he never made that sort of point."

"What sort of things did he say?" Maggie asked. "I don't think we discussed that with everything that happened."

Ruby set her coffee down and folded her hands. "He talked about having a uniform message at each and every point of customer contact, whether that was in a brick and mortar setting or an online presence," she said. "He actually spoke against using gimmicks that did not reflect the mission of the business, whatever that might be."

"Sounds to me like he needed to heed his own advice," Brett said.

The waitress returned then with another server and began passing out large platters of food. Maggie handed a second plate of pancakes over to Brett, then chuckled when he grinned. "You must be pretty hungry," she teased.

"Yeah, my old lady feeds me on day-old donuts and leftover coffee," he said with a grin. He leaned his shoulder into Maggie and kissed the side of her head.

"You wish you got old donuts and coffee from me," Maggie said. She tossed half of her biscuit at him.

"I think this is why we came," Orson added suddenly.

"What's that, Orson?" Brooks asked.

"This." Orson pointed to Maggie and Brett. "We don't do this enough."

For the following half hour or so, they chatted easily and ate. Maggie refilled her coffee twice. Brett finished his large stack of pancakes, then began teasing her for a bite of hers. She fended off his fork with her own.

"What are we going to do after this?" Myra asked.

"I don't think we've given that too much thought, to be honest," Ruby said. "There is a shopping district not far from here we can check out."

Maggie turned her attention to the inside of the restaurant. She wanted to find a restroom. "I'll be right back," she announced and stood up. Brett stood and moved out of her way to let her out of the booth.

Maggie wound her way through the middle of the restaurant. She turned sideways around tables and chairs and found her way to the restrooms on the other side. When she was finished, she peered at her reflection for a moment and decided the time away had already done her some good.

When she exited the short hall that led to the bathrooms, Maggie stood and surveyed the room, hoping to find a simpler way back to her table. Instead of cutting through the middle, she walked in a large circle along the room. A short wall separated the main dining area from the smaller section with the windows where they were seated. Two smaller booths were placed against the wall. As she walked closer, Maggie noticed a woman seated alone in one of the booths. She averted her eyes so as not to stare but looked up slightly when she walked past. The woman was cutting into a short stack of pancakes as she passed by. Her short dark hair and waiflike complexion reminded her of someone.

Maggie slid back into her spot at their table when it hit her. "I think I just saw Rebecca Concord," she announced to Ruby.

"Where?" Ruby asked, looking around.

Maggie pointed in the direction of the wall. "Over there, eating alone," she said. The woman was partially visible from where they were seated.

Ruby looked for a long time and then nodded her head slowly. "That is her," she said. "I'm quite sure of it."

Maggie thought little more about it. The conversation turned to the activities planned for the remainder of the day. "I say we return to the cabin and take a nap," Orson said.

"You know, I don't disagree," Brooks said. He pushed back from the table and sighed, patting his stomach. "I don't remember the last time I ate that many carbs in one sitting."

"Looks like you're carrying the next little one already." Orson chuckled. He reached over and patted Brooks on the stomach.

"So, what do we say, gang?" Brett asked. "Are we going shopping or are we heading back to the cabin for a nap?"

Before anyone could answer, a small group of women moved noisily through the front of the restaurant. Two servers followed them. A middle-aged woman with long, bleached blonde hair dressed in black silk from her blouse and skirt to the spiky heels on her feet, appeared to be the leader of the pack. She pushed her way around chairs and tables. Maggie watched in awe as the woman made her way through the restaurant toward the back. Two other women, both around the same age, followed right behind her. None of them seemed too concerned about the other patrons whose meals they interrupted as they pushed through them.

"Ma'am, you can't just walk through here when we have other people waiting in front of you," one of the servers said when they were within earshot of the table.

"I'm not eating here," the first woman said. She swung her long hair over her shoulder.

"Then you're going to have to leave," the second server said. Maggie wondered if he was a manager of some sort. "You are disturbing our customers."

"I'm not here for your other customers," the

woman said. "Only this one." She stopped close to the short wall where Rebecca was seated.

"Ma'am, you cannot be in here and you cannot continue to disturb our guests." The young manager stood between the set of booths and the women.

"We no longer require your assistance." A redheaded woman behind the blonde stepped forward and stood in front of the manager.

"You need to leave this second," he responded. He kept his voice low, but Maggie could hear every word he spoke. The entire table had gone quiet.

"We are not going to leave," the first woman said. "And unless you want this to turn into a scene for the entire place to witness, you need to back off and let me say what I have come to say to this woman. After that, we will leave. No questions asked."

"I'm calling the police," the manager said.

"You do what you have to do," the redhead said. "By the time they get here, this will be over and done with anyway."

The manager sighed and pulled the server with him back toward the front. Maggie wondered if he planned to call the police anyway.

"Should we interfere?" Brooks looked up and asked Brett.

"Not yet," Brett said. He watched the situation

with keen interest. "We aren't anywhere near our own jurisdictions. But if things start to get out of hand, it's a matter of duty I think."

"Deal," Brooks said and turned his attention back to the women.

"Rebecca Concord," the blonde said. "It's all your fault my husband died yesterday."

CHAPTER NINE

Maggie nearly choked on her coffee when the blonde spoke. She strained slightly to hear what she had to say over her own coughing.

"I'm sorry. I think you have the wrong person," Rebecca said in a meek voice.

"Oh, please. You know full well what I'm talking about," the blonde snapped.

"She's Cathy Riles, and you're the reason her husband is dead," the redhead repeated.

Cathy glared at the woman over her shoulder. "Let's not inform the rest of the world who I am while we're at it," she said.

"Sorry," the redhead said.

Cathy turned back to Rebecca. "You know what you did," she said. "You didn't do the one job you were hired to do, and now one of those floozies has killed my husband. This is all your fault."

"That isn't fair," Rebecca said. Her voice raised a little when she spoke, but her words still sounded thin and hollow.

"Your one job was to manage things for him," Cathy continued. "That's all you had to do, and you blew it!"

"My job was to assist him, and that's what I did," Rebecca replied. "Now if you don't mind, I have somewhere to be."

"Where would that be? Have you already found another woman's husband to attach yourself to like a barnacle on a ship?" the redhead asked. She looked to Cathy for approval.

Cathy nodded and smiled at the redhead. "That's a good point, Stacey," she said. "Have you found another rich married man to go and work for already? If you have, please give me his number so I can reach out to his wife and warn her about what she's about to deal with."

"And what do you think that's going to be, Cathy?" Rebecca asked. She stood up slightly from her seat. The angles of her thin, willowy body hardened as she leaned over the table. "I was hired by

Stanley to be his personal assistant, and I performed those duties very well."

"I bet you performed very well," Stacey snickered. "Just not in the way you wanted to."

"Be quiet," Cathy hissed her disapproval. Stacey hung her head.

"You didn't have an affair with Stanley, as much as we all know that's what you wanted more than anything, but you did a poor job of keeping him from other women," Cathy said. "And that was your job."

"No, it wasn't," Rebecca replied. "It never was my job! If your late husband was unfaithful, that has nothing to do with me. It was his problem and your problem, and it has nothing to do with the work I performed for him."

"You ladies need to shut up and leave the rest of us in peace," an older man seated at a table close by spoke up. His words were followed by a round of applause from half of the people around him.

"Shut your mouth, old man," Stacey said. Maggie wondered if she was the intimidator of the little group.

"The police are on their way," the young manager called from the front of the restaurant.

Cathy appeared to ignore their words. "I want to know what you plan to do to make this right."

"Nothing," Rebecca said. She stood up fully and picked up a small purse next to her. She walked out of the booth seat and pushed her way around Cathy, bumping slightly into Stacey.

"Ouch! You just assaulted me," the redhead shouted.

"Good!" Rebecca headed straight for the front of the restaurant.

"She sure changed," Ruby said when the front doors opened, and Rebecca walked out.

"What do you mean?" Myra asked.

"That was not the same woman who tried to intimidate us into staying in the class at the convention," Ruby said.

"Yeah, that woman acted like she had a screw loose," Maggie said. "Or two or three."

"She sounded pretty normal to me," Orson said.

"That's the problem." Ruby frowned and looked at her friends.

"Are we all ready to go?" Myra asked. Brooks stood up and led the rest of them out of the booth. They walked to the front and quickly settled the bill, then exited through the front door. Maggie looked around immediately for any signs of the women from before. But they appeared to be gone.

Maggie wanted to feel something compassionate

for the woman named Cathy. After all, she had just lost her husband. But her behavior made it hard to see her as a grieving widow. Instead, she seemed harsh and cruel, entitled, and accusing.

Her sympathies were more directed at Rebecca. It was difficult to know which Rebecca she felt the most sympathy for, the normal sounding and acting woman they had just seen attacked, or the oddly behaving, robotic-speaking person from the day before. Either way, the woman had been through something.

On her way to the truck, Maggie spotted Rebecca leaning against the side of the restaurant. She reached for Brett's hand, squeezed it quickly, and then released it. She walked slowly toward the thin woman.

"Are you alright?" she asked timidly. "We were just inside and witnessed what happened. Are you okay?"

Rebecca looked at her and dropped her eyes. "I'm fine," she said. "I just want to return to my hotel."

"Do you need help? Or are you waiting for a ride?" Maggie asked.

Rebecca nodded. "I ordered an Uber," she said and checked the screen of her phone. "The driver should be here in a couple of minutes."

Maggie nodded and smiled in her direction. "Forgive the intrusion," she said. "I just wanted to check on you."

Rebecca stared at her for a second. Maggie thought she then looked directly at Ruby, but she couldn't tell. Her eyes narrowed and the muscles in her face seemed to tighten. "You were there," she said. The robotic cadence returned. "You were at the convention. With Stanley. You shouldn't be here."

"Maggie, let's go," Brett whispered in her hair. He pulled slightly on her arm. "I don't like where this is going."

Maggie allowed herself to be led away. She opened her hand up and threaded her fingers between Brett's as they walked toward the truck.

CHAPTER TEN

"We still don't know what we're doing the rest of the day," Brett said. He stepped out of the truck when they arrived back at the log cabin.

"Why don't we all head inside for a moment and we can make up our minds, then?" Myra suggested. She headed for the cabin with Brooks behind her.

Orson disappeared as soon as they were all inside. "I wonder if Orson decided to take a nap?" Naomi asked quietly when they were gathered in the kitchen together.

"I wonder if this whole trip is a bit much for him," Maggie asked. She leaned against the stove and folded her arms. Maybe she had missed signs back home in Dogwood Mountain before they came out. She felt a deep pit in her middle when she thought of something happening to him, especially if it was her fault.

Orson reappeared in the kitchen then. He had changed into a pair of sleek blue jogging pants, topped with a white t-shirt and a matching blue jacket. He walked past Brett and Maggie and began opening up the cabinets.

"Is there something you are looking for?" Myra asked him.

"Yep," he said without turning around to look at her.

"Can I help you?" Ruby asked.

"Nope," Orson replied. He opened the door to a cabinet and pulled out a small tumbler. He set the glass down on the counter and removed a short, round bottle from his jacket. He pulled off the wax seal, twisted off the cap, and slowly tipped the neck of the bottle over the tumbler until it was halfway filled with amber liquid. Orson turned around from the counter with the glass in his hand. "If you all need me," he said, lifting the glass and then the bottle. "I'll be outside." He grinned and headed straight for the back door.

"Wait," Maggie said. "Are you feeling alright? Do you need us to stay here with you?"

Orson sipped from the glass and winked at her. "I

feel pretty good, but I'm about to feel a whole lot better," he said. "I'm going to go out that door and head right down to those chairs you all were sitting in last night with my two friends here. I am going to look at that view and listen to the trees and hope I get to meet a bear before Ruby does." He smiled again and headed outside.

"Y'all, I think he's going to be just fine," Brett said after Orson made his way to the fire pit area outside.

"Apparently." Maggie laughed.

"Okay, what if the rest of us go to that shopping district we were talking about and walk around for a little while?" Brooks suggested. "Because you all know that we cannot head back home at the end of the week without spending all our money on flimsy trinkets."

"Of course not." Ruby grinned. "I know I have some shopping to do for a couple of kids in my life as well."

"Yeah, and one of us has three grown daughters who expect something little and artisanal," Brett said.

"Wait, Ruby. You're shopping for Wyatt, too? I want to make sure you don't get him the same thing I'm going to get him." Brett's voice trailed off as he went out the door after Ruby. Maggie was the last one in the kitchen. She shook her head and laughed at the thought of her grandson being the subject of a shopping rivalry between two friends.

Ruby had climbed into the back of the pickup behind the driver's seat when Maggie reached the driveway. She glanced toward Orson, who had already made himself comfortable near the fire pit. Naomi rode with Brooks and Myra this time. Maggie halfway wondered if Naomi was steering clear of Ruby, so she was less likely to have a run in with any bears.

When they pulled into the parking area, Maggie was grateful Brett had decided to drive. They drove around for several minutes before they found a parking space. She felt a twinge of excitement. The thought of shopping just for fun sounded like a welcome change.

The sun shone brightly overhead when they walked toward the shopping center. Cool winds blew down from the mountains. Despite the sun shining overhead, the air was crisp and cool and rich with the aroma of baked apples and cinnamon.

They headed first to a small store decorated like a medieval Celtic cottage. Rich scents wafted from the store. Maggie picked up a bar of goat's milk soap and sniffed. She was enthralled by the floor-length knitted cardigans and wispy broom skirts.

"Help me pick something out for the girls," Brett leaned over to her and said. "Please. I am begging you to help me find something three young adult women would like."

Maggie laughed aloud and patted him on the arm. "Come with me," she said. She led him around the store. They filled a shopping basket with skirts, sweaters, and a pair of leggings for each. Maggie added a bar of scented soap and a matching candle for good measure.

"You sure they are going to like this stuff?" Brett asked her at the register.

Maggie nodded. "I am one hundred percent sure they will like it," she reassured him as they left the medieval cottage and headed into the main part of the shopping center. They passed a quaint donut shop, which sent Maggie into a fit of giggles.

"I do want to visit the coffee shop while we are here," Ruby announced.

"There's a coffee shop? Is it close?" Brett asked.

"It's an amazing place and it's right there." Ruby pointed and led the way inside. "I've ordered coffee from them for years, but I have never been able to visit in person."

Just outside the coffee shop, after they finished shopping, Maggie spotted the blonde from the pancake house. "That's Stanley's wife over there, isn't it?"

Brooks nodded. "It sure looks like her."

"And that looks like it could be the redhead she was with, too," Myra said, nodding toward a woman with her back to them.

They watched her quietly for several moments. Cathy stood in the center of a group of other women. She held a gaudy, rhinestone-bedazzled purse over her head and cheered. "I got it, I got it," she chanted after the cheer. She had changed her clothes since her exhibition at the pancake house. Her jeans were painted-on tight, and her black blouse sparkled with the same bedazzled gaudiness as the handbag.

Maggie was unsure what the fuss was all about, but she was quite sure the woman was not behaving like a someone grieving the loss of her husband. It was odd to Maggie that she would carry on in that way in public. It was hard to really say, because she had never lost a spouse. Aside from losing her great-aunt Marjorie, she had not experienced a close relative death in some time.

The woman cheered louder. One produced an extra-large wine glass covered in sparkly sequins. The redheaded friend held the goblet up and gestured drinking from it. "She's single again," she sang, horribly loud and off-key. "Hold onto your men!"

"Look out, ladies, she's single again," the rest sang in chorus.

"I think we ought to get out of here," Brett suggested. "I had an idea about something we can do together tomorrow."

Without a word, they turned and headed back toward the parking lot.

"So, what's this grand plan you have for tomorrow, Brett," Ruby asked when they returned to the cabin.

Orson was seated inside the kitchen on the bar stool. His whiskey bottle was a third less full than it had been before they left. His eyes sparked with humor and mischief as he spoke. "What's that Sheriff? Are you gonna take us up in the mountains to be your posse looking for the bad guys?"

"I think someone has had quite the day already," Myra said.

"If by someone you mean this old man, my darling adopted daughter, you would be right," Orson answered.

"You know, I think you ought to go off to bed for a nice long nap," Brooks suggested.

Orson's head swiveled toward him. "Oh, I will, Son," he smiled generously. "And you're going to help me get there. But before I go, I wanna hear the lawman's plan for tomorrow."

Brett chuckled and cleared his throat. He sat down on the stool next to Orson's and tapped the counter top with his finger. "There's a train that goes through the mountains," he said. "It is an old fashioned train, and it winds around through the trees and over a river."

"Sold!" Orson slapped the countertop loudly with the palm of his hand. Brett nearly jumped out of his chair.

"You haven't heard everything else about it," Myra said.

"Don't need to," Orson said. "You all just let me know when I need to have my shoes on, and I'll be there." He slid down off of the stool, holding onto the counter with both hands to steady himself. "In the meantime, Brooks, my boy, help an old man to his room for a little nighty-night."

CHAPTER ELEVEN

"How far is it to this train station?" Orson asked from the backseat of the pickup. Maggie glanced at Brett and bit her lip to hold in the giggles. Before Orson had emerged from his room that morning, a rigorous discussion had taken place out on the deck about who he would ride with. In the end, it was decided that since he rode in with Myra and Brooks, he should spend a little more time with Brett and Maggie.

"The train station is about an hour away," Brett said patiently.

Orson shifted in his seat. "Have either of you ever been on an old fashioned locomotive before? They can be smelly and dirty and loud."

"If you didn't want to go, you could have stayed behind at the cabin," Maggie said gently.

"Yeah, I know," Orson said. He sighed loudly and placed both hands on the backs of their seats. "Listen, I'm not irritated that we're going, but I have a heck of a headache from my escapades yesterday. Maybe I should have stayed behind, not for my sake, but for everyone else's."

Maggie's heart melted a little at his words. "Nonsense, Orson," she said, patting his hand. "We wouldn't want to go without you."

"If you were smart you would," he said, sitting back. "But I thank you for the sentiment."

Maggie said nothing but reached into her purse for her favorite headache medicine. "Take this," she instructed him. "You will feel better before we board the train."

Orson swallowed the medicine and turned to gaze out of the windows for the remainder of the journey there. Maggie turned back and rode silently next to Brett, her hand entwined in his for most of the trip.

"Look at this place," she said when they arrived at their destination. They walked across a path to a quaint small town train depot. She heard the low whistle of a train when she entered the small gift shop.

"Do we want to grab a snack before we head out?" Orson asked behind her.

"Are you hungry? They serve lunch on the train," she told him.

Orson shrugged. "I feel a little famished," he said. "I think I'll grab some trail mix and some juice."

Maggie walked around the gift shop and glanced at the clock on the wall above the cash register. She wanted to get out to the train as soon as the boarding call came. While she was sure she would not be allowed to board before that time, she wanted to drink the experience in, from the train whistle to the burst of steam from the engine.

She decided to make her purchases after they returned from the trip. She headed back outside and after a short time, Maggie heard the whistle blow and the announcement of the boarding call. The journey would take them around a large mountain gorge, stopping halfway at a riverfront trading post and gift shop.

Everyone lined up to board and as promised, the train itself was reminiscent of the turn of the last century. They had chosen the closed coach for their journey. Once inside, she chose a seat next to Brett. The seats were arranged in groups of four, with two looking forward and two facing backward. Maggie sat next to the window. Orson took one seat facing them. Myra and Brooks sat across the aisle with Naomi and Ruby facing the two of them.

After several moments, a train employee instructed them about the bathrooms and announced the meal schedule. Maggie listened impatiently. She was eager to feel the rails under their seats. At last, the stewardess was replaced by a live banjo and a folk singer. The train began rolling and their trip was underway. Maggie smiled and snuggled into Brett's arm when the train pulled away from the small town and the mountains came fully into view.

The first half of the trip passed quickly. Maggie didn't talk much while they wound through the mountains. She was far too enamored with the sights to speak. Brett seemed to be similarly enthralled. He leaned over her shoulder and gazed out the window for most of the trip.

Before the train began to slow down for the stop at the trading post, Brett announced his need to get up and stretch his legs. He rose and kissed Maggie on top of her head. Just past the small corridor to the bathrooms another door led outside to the rear platform, a small, railed balcony where passengers could stand and take in the outdoors. "I might spend a minute or two out there, just getting a little fresh air," he told her. She wondered if he was experiencing some sort of nausea from the trip.

A moment after he headed down the aisle toward

the bathroom, Orson stood up from his seat and plopped down next to her.

"You are a lucky woman," he said as soon as he sat down.

"Random," Maggie teased him. "What inspired that?

Orson shrugged his shoulders. "I guess it's thinking about Myra and Brooks, and how lucky they are to have found each other in their young lives," he said. "Naomi and Ruby are alone. I have Gretchen, but I'm a lot older than any of you."

She leaned over and planted a kiss on his weathered cheek.

"It's wonderful how all of you scooped up this bitter, lonely old man and made a family out of it," Orson said. "You married young like Myra and Brooks, and it turned out to be a mistake. But look at you now. Here you have found the love of your life in the middle of your life. That is a priceless gift."

"You aren't wrong," Maggie said. "But you do know we all love you, right? You're like our father, our grumpy, cantankerous, darling father."

Orson chuckled and patted her arm. "I'm grateful for the family I have been blessed with," he said and rose to move back to his seat.

Brett returned a few minutes later. "Lunch is on

the way," he said. "I'm glad. I need something to drink."

"Are you feeling alright?" she asked him.

Brett glanced over at Orson first, then turned to her and smiled. "I just have some butterflies in my stomach, that's all," he said.

Maggie winked over at Ruby when the boxed lunch was served a short time later. She opened the thin cardboard box to reveal a small lunch. It was very good food, but she felt a surge of pride in the boxed lunches Ruby concocted at the donut shop. Of course, it would have been impossible to reconstruct such a meal on a moving train. And she was grateful for the lunch when she was finished.

"I'm glad we haven't run into those people from breakfast," Myra whispered across the aisle a little while later. "Once was enough."

"Don't speak so soon," Orson announced. He had just returned to his seat from the restroom.

"What are you talking about?" Brett asked him.

"Back there," Orson said and jerked his head toward the car behind them. "In that open air car. I saw the other woman from the pancake house. She's back there riding all alone."

"Wait a minute," Brooks leaned over and said. "You saw her? You're sure?"

Orson nodded. "I spotted her when I was out on the rear platform and the door came open," he said. "Let's just hope Maggie here doesn't decide now is the time to investigate."

CHAPTER TWELVE

The train began to slow down just after Orson spoke. Maggie felt butterflies of her own when she considered what a confrontation might look like, but she told herself there was a good chance they wouldn't even run into each other.

The train rolled to a stop at last. Maggie could hear the rush of the wide river as soon as the steam engine came to a loud stop. She stood, grabbed Brett's hand, and followed him out of the car. His skin was cold and clammy. She stopped him just outside of the trading post.

"Honey, are you getting sick? You feel like you might have a fever."

Brett smiled at her, a little sadly, and rested his

hands on her shoulder. "I just have something on my mind, that's all," he said.

"Maggie, look!" Ruby called out a little ahead of them. Maggie, followed by Brett, rushed over to see what the fuss was all about. "At last! And there is an entire family of them!"

A large black bear scampered after three small cubs on the riverbank on the other side. Ruby moved down to the edge, as close as she could get without getting in, and watched them play for several moments.

"This is really neat," Brett said while they watched. Maggie looked over at him. His color had returned a little. She wondered if he had just needed some fresh air.

"I'm going to head over to the trading post," Maggie said after a moment. "I need to use the restroom."

"That's fine," Ruby answered. "We'll be along in a soon."

Maggie walked back up the bank toward the sidewalk that led to the large gift shop. She glanced back once at Ruby and Brett and wondered what had the two of them in such an intense conversation. She walked to the other side of the large gift shop. Orson found her first.

"You see anything the kids might like?" he asked her.

"I haven't even looked around much yet," she said. "I'm looking for the bathroom."

Maggie headed to the other side of the building. She found the restroom quickly and freshened up. When she emerged, she spotted everyone else, aside from Orson, gathered in a small huddle in a corner. She felt instant concern, based on the looks on their faces, and headed straight for them.

"What is going on over here?" she whispered to Ruby when she caught up.

"Where's Orson?" was her reply.

"I think I saw him going toward the snack section," Maggie said.

"Well, we need to decide if we want to head back to our seats now," Ruby said.

"Why? We're supposed to be here for at least an hour. What's going on?" Maggie asked. She looked around for signs of danger but saw nothing.

"Look," Ruby whispered. She nodded in the direction of the postcard display. "We just spotted Cathy and her buddy."

Maggie looked but could not see either of the women. "Are you sure?" she asked.

"We all saw her," Naomi leaned in and confirmed.

"What I want to know is how these people keep showing up wherever we go," Brooks said. He ran his hand over his head. "I just don't get it. Coincidence? The universe's wonderful sense of humor?"

"We have no idea what might happen with them."

"There is no reason to think that anything actually will," Brooks said.

"Actually, there might be," Myra told her husband. She pointed outside the large windows where Rebecca walked toward the trading post. She was headed right to the door just ten feet from where the other women stood.

"This might not be good," Brett said.

"Maybe we ought to find security or something," Naomi suggested.

"Or we can just stay back and let them figure it out on their own," Orson said behind her. Maggie turned and smiled, grateful they were all together.

"Let's just all go and get our shopping done and head back to the train," Brooks suggested. "We don't need to worry about whatever is going on with those people."

Maggie nodded and began searching the toy section for something appropriate for a child. She found a large, very realistic stuffed black bear and decided to pick one up for Wyatt. She walked a few steps away, then turned back and picked up two more, one for Lexi and one for Ruby.

"That's a lot of bears, ma'am," Brett said when he caught up to her at the cashier. He held a quilt in his hands, a hand sewn tapestry of the river and the trading post.

"What do you have there?" Maggie asked.

"Just something to remember this place by," Brett said. "Would you like to walk along the river with me for another few minutes before we get back on the train?"

Maggie felt her heart sink. She was starting to think Brett was about to make a dreadful revelation to her.

Was he sick? Leaving her? Or maybe he had taken another job out of state and wanted this trip to work up the courage to tell her. Before she could think another terrible thought, she heard a scream from the far end of the trading post. She closed her eyes and turned, confident the shouting involved Cathy and Rebecca.

"Oh, knock off the act," Cathy yelled. She stood about two feet from the younger woman. Her finger was shoved in Rebecca's face, just inches from her nose.

"It isn't an act," Rebecca said.

"Really? How do you explain the fact that you can act completely normal, and then go on like a robotic idiot the next?" Stacey chimed in.

"Just go away and leave me alone," Rebecca said in her normal voice. She turned to walk away from the women.

"I think it's time for us to go, too," Brett said. He took her hand and headed back to the train. As they were leaving, they spotted a couple of uniformed officers approach the women.

"Good," Maggie said. "Maybe that will be resolved." They headed outside and walked down the sidewalk.

"Hey, folks," a uniformed train conductor approached them. "Are you all from the train?" he asked them.

Brett nodded quickly. "I'm going to ask you to go on and board again. It seems we have a security issue and we have been asked to head back in the next five minutes."

He nodded toward them and headed inside the trading post.

"Well," Brett said, gazing down at the river. "So much for that idea."

CHAPTER THIRTEEN

"I wonder how they made sure everyone who was supposed to got back on the train?" Myra asked a few minutes later. They had all rushed back to their seats. Maggie spotted a couple of uniformed police officers among them.

"I don't know, but I don't want this trip to be ruined because of those women," Brooks said. "Maybe the police will investigate the two of them," Brooks said.

"You don't know they haven't," Myra said.

"Based on how often we've seen all of them, I'm going to guess that they haven't," Brooks replied.

Brett leaned forward to comment but was cut off by a loud commotion before he could speak. Rebecca burst into the car and rushed halfway down the aisle. Maggie rose up out of her seat and stared at her.

"You," Rebecca said, pointing at her. "You know who I'm looking for! Tell me if you've seen them!"

Maggie shook her head. "Just at the river like everyone else," she said. "Why don't you go back to your seat and settle down."

Rebecca shook her head. "I am done," she said. "This ends now!"

"I have no idea what you're talking about," Maggie said. "But whatever it is, you can resolve it later. These people here just want a safe ride back to the depot."

"What's going on?" Brett whispered in her ear.

"Gun," Maggie said quietly. She stared at the black metal object in Rebecca's hand.

"There she is!" This time, the shouting came from the other end of the train car. Maggie wanted to cover her face with the palm of her hand and scream. Why wouldn't these women just leave each other alone?

"You," Rebecca hissed. "You ruined my life! How could you do it?"

Maggie turned around to see Cathy standing behind a pair of police officers. Her redheaded friend stood next to her.

"I have no idea what you are talking about,

Rebecca." Cathy smirked. "But I do know your secret and I am going to share it with the rest of the world if you don't admit you killed my husband!"

"Too late," Stacey sang. She smiled and held a cell phone up in the air.

"What are you doing with my phone?" Cathy asked her.

"Only what you and Stanley should have done forever ago," she said.

"You didn't," Rebecca screamed. She raised the gun and pointed it directly at Cathy and Stacey. Both officers quickly drew their weapons. Maggie pulled her own phone out and began searching for anything she could find under Rebecca's name. She was sure that whatever Stacey had done, she would find it linked to the blonde's social media accounts. People like her always wanted to be in the limelight.

"Oh, no," she said and sank into her seat.

"What is it?" Brett asked. His eyes darted between her and the situation going on around them.

Maggie silently turned her phone screen toward him. Stacey's name was actually Anastasia Hibbard, and she had indeed published something on social media, an unforgiving social media profile starring Rebecca Concord.

"He held that over my head for the past five

years," Rebecca said suddenly. Maggie rose up and turned to look at her. "Don't tell me you didn't just find it. I saw you pull out your phone."

"I did," Maggie said. "But I don't think it's terrible enough for you to be holding a gun on a crowded train car. You don't want to hurt any of these people."

"I don't care who gets hurt," Rebecca replied in her robotic voice.

"Oh, knock it off," Cathy said in disgust. "We all know it's an act."

"Maybe not," Brett said. He rose up next to Maggie with his hands out in front of him. "If your late husband really was holding something over her head, she might have developed an emotional response to it."

"What are you, a head shrink?" Stacey asked him.

"No, I'm actually a county sheriff back home in Missouri, and I have dealt with things like this before," Brett said slowly.

"That's what is going on here, isn't it?" Maggie piped up. "Right, Rebecca?"

Rebecca nodded her head. "Stanley held the secrets of my past over my head for years, and forced me to do many things for him," she said.

"Including covering up his faithfulness to me," Cathy shouted.

Rebecca nodded her head. "Yes, including that," she said. "You have no idea what he put me through."

"And you killed him, didn't you?" Cathy asked. "You killed my husband because of your secrets!"

"Yes! Yes I killed him," Rebecca screamed. "I killed him, and I don't regret it!" She held the gun up again.

"But you don't need to hurt anyone else," Maggie said. She stood up and raised her hands high above her head.

"Maggie!" Brett hissed.

"I don't want to hurt anyone, no," Rebecca said. "I just want to be left alone."

"You aren't going to be left alone," Stacey said. "You are going to go to prison for the rest of your life!"

"Okay, just settle down," Cathy said. Maggie turned toward her. Her face had paled considerably. "You actually admitted to killing him."

Rebecca nodded her head. Her arms lowered slightly. "I'm sorry! I didn't want to hurt anyone, but I couldn't take it anymore," she said. "I'd been slowly poisoning him for weeks."

"Okay, let's just all calm down," one of the offi-cers spoke up at last.

"Rebecca," Maggie said. "Why don't you set the gun down and let these officers help you? What's done is done. And I know you don't want to make it any worse."

"Why don't you sit down and shut up?" Stacey glared at Maggie. "Nobody asked you to be a part of this."

"Shut up, Stacey," Cathy said.

"Why don't shut up for a change?" Stacey shouted. "You told me Rebecca did you a favor killing your husband. You just wanted her to admit it so the cops wouldn't think otherwise and mess up his life insurance!"

Maggie was vaguely aware of movement beside her. She looked over in time to see Brett and Brooks moving swiftly down the aisle toward Rebecca. Before the rest of the passengers could collectively gasp, Brooks had Rebecca's hand pointing up in the air. He held her there while Brett pried the gun from her fingers. He immediately released the clip and removed a round from the chamber. He turned the gun around and held it out to the approaching officer with his hand.

Seconds later, the officers marched Rebecca off of

the train in handcuffs. Brooks and Brett were rewarded with a round of applause from the grateful passengers and returned to their seats.

Orson shook his head at the two of them. "We can't take you three anywhere," he said. "You always have to play cops and robbers."

CHAPTER FOURTEEN

Maggie woke early the next morning and headed outside to take in the final day of their vacation. They'd decided to head home early and leave at the same time Brooks and Myra had planned to. Despite the unfortunate murder of Stanley Riles and the arrest of Rebecca Concord for his death, their short time away in the Smoky Mountains had a worked its magic on her spirit.

She wanted one more quiet mountain morning with the mist rising high into the atmosphere before they headed back home, back to work, and back to normal life. She held a cup of coffee in her hands as she made her way to the circle of chairs around the fire pit. There was a nip of cool night air still hanging around. She raised the mug to her lips and blew lightly over the top. She inhaled the slight cherry scent from Ruby's beloved Smoky Mountain coffee blend and sipped slowly. She had to admit, there was something a little different in the air. She felt something shift in her own head. It was a feeling she planned to carry home when they headed back to Missouri.

Brooks and Myra got some much needed rest, and of course, Ruby saw her beloved bears. Naomi appeared to have relaxed as well, and she was happy about the additional responsibilities awaiting her when they returned. She wondered if they would ever see Naomi happy in a relationship, but it was really none of her business in the end.

The biggest change of all had come to Orson. The color in his cheeks seemed to return. She figured the time in the mountain air had done its magic, but by far the biggest effect came when he announced his desire to cut his hours at the donut shop back to just fifteen every week. He planned to make it in a few hours each day and work until lunch, after which he would retire to the Old timer's table, or out to the lake with his fishing pole, or even back home to the hammock Brooks promised to set up for him in the backyard.

She heard the door shut quietly and looked up to

see Brett smiling as he descended the steps to join her. He carried two cups of coffee. "I brought you out a cup," he said sheepishly. "I guess I should have known you would have already had one in your hands."

"I won't turn down a second cup. Mine is already almost gone and that saves me from having to go get more myself."

"I guess that means I'm still the hero in this story, after all," Brett said. He set the coffee down on the wide wooden arm of her chair and took a seat next to her. "Are you drinking in the last moments before we have to head back home?"

"Something like that," Maggie said. She reached for his hand and held it softly. "What about you, Brett? I was just sitting here thinking about how good this week has been for everyone else, but I don't know how you feel."

Brett gazed at her then looked up toward the mountains. He exhaled slowly and nodded. "I love it here," he said. "I love the Ozarks, but this is a special place. And I hope that it will always have a special meaning for me, for the rest of my life."

"That's a big ask for such a short stay." Maggie was slightly confused by his meaning.

"Well, there's still one memory I hope to make."

Maggie looked over at him, still unsure what he meant. "I'm sorry, sweetheart," she said, shaking her head slightly. "But you have totally lost me."

Brett leaned back and closed his eyes. "That's a shame, because keeping you is precisely what I mean to do."

Maggie sat upright in her chair. She placed one hand over his forehead and felt for signs of a fever. "Are you feeling alright?"

Brett opened his eyes and smiled. "I am. I'm a little off lately, but you still love me anyway, right?"

"Of course I do," Maggie said. "What brought this on all of a sudden?"

Brett pushed himself up by his elbows and turned to look at her. "A little while back you weren't sure if a life with me was what you wanted."

Maggie studied his face for a moment, and then spoke. "That's not exactly true," she said. "I wasn't sure if I wanted to ever be married again."

"And now?" he asked. His eyes filled suddenly with tears. "Now how do you feel? Because that is a very important question in my head right now."

Maggie sighed. She looked toward the mountain again, then down at his fingers as he threaded them through hers. A life with Brett? Why had she just assumed she would have that anyway, whether they were married or not?

"How do I feel about marriage in general, or marriage with you?" Maggie asked.

"With me," Brett said. His voice was husky and deep as he spoke. "Because, I have a very important question I want you to answer."

Looking back, it may have been the lack of panic in her gut that made the magic the most magical. She felt herself filled with warmth seeping into every cranny of her soul. She felt the sweetness of it and smiled. Suddenly the secrecy with Ruby made sense.

"Marriage with you? Marriage with you would be the best end for my beginning, Brett Mission," she said. "I think I would happily spend the rest of my life as your wife."

"I am so glad you said that," Brett said. "Because since the moment I set eyes on you when you returned to Dogwood Mountain, I've known…"

"Oh, for Pete's sake, just pull out the ring and pop the question already!"

Maggie swiveled her head around and looked up at the deck. Orson stood in the middle between Naomi and Myra, who were flanked on either side by Ruby and Brooks. "We aren't getting any younger up here."

Maggie turned back to Brett. Tears flowed freely down her cheeks, half from the realization that he was about to ask her to marry him, and the other half from laughter. Brett looked up at the deck and gestured with two fingers in front of his eyes. "I am watching you, old man," he said, turning his fingers toward Orson.

"And we're all watching you, boy, so get on with it," Orson grumbled. Maggie noted the smile playing on the corner of his mouth.

"Maggie Sharpe," Brett said when she turned back around. He held a diamond ring close to her. "Will you be my wife?"

Maggie looked back at the deck. She gazed at each of her friends. Her eyes stopped on Ruby, her best friend, who nodded her smiling face slightly in encouragement. She looked back at Brett and smiled through her tears.

"Yes," she said. "Nothing would make me happier."

If you enjoyed Baking Matters Worse, check out the next book in the series, Tough As They Crumb, today!

AUTHOR'S NOTE

I'd love to hear your thoughts on my books, the storylines, and anything else that you'd like to comment on—reader feedback is very important to me. My contact information, along with some other helpful links, is listed on the next page. If you'd like to be on my list of "folks to contact" with updates, release and sales notifications, etc.… just shoot me an email and let me know. Thanks for reading!

Also…

… if you're looking for more great reads, Summer Prescott Books publishes several popular series by outstanding Cozy Mystery authors.

CONTACT SUMMER PRESCOTT
BOOKS PUBLISHING

Blog and Book Catalog: http:// summerprescottbooks.com
Email: summer.prescott.cozies@gmail.com

And...be sure to check out the Summer Prescott Cozy Mysteries fan page and Summer Prescott Books Publishing Page on Facebook – let's be friends!

To sign up for our fun and exciting newsletter, which will give you opportunities to win prizes and swag, enter contests, and be the first to know about New Releases, click here: http://summerprescottbooks.com

Made in United States
North Haven, CT
15 March 2023

34102871R00065